SHORT TALES

NORSE MYTHS

LOKI

Adapted by
Rob M. Worley

Illustrated by
Brandon McKinney

visit us at www.abdopublishing.com

Published by Magic Wagon, a division of the ABDO Publishing Group, 8000 West 78th Street, Edina, Minnesota, 55439. Copyright © 2011 by Abdo Consulting Group, Inc. International copyrights reserved in all countries. All rights reserved. No part of this book may be reproduced in any form without written permission from the publisher.

Short Tales ™ is a trademark and logo of Magic Wagon.

Printed in the United States of America, North Mankato, Minnesota.
032010
092010
This book contains at least 10% recycled materials.

Adapted Text by Rob M. Worley
Illustrations by Brandon McKinney
Colors by Wes Hartman
Edited by Stephanie Hedlund
Interior Layout by Kristen Fitzner Denton
Book Design and Packaging by Shannon Eric Denton

Library of Congress Cataloging-in-Publication Data

Worley, Rob M.
  Loki / adapted by Rob M. Worley ; illustrated by Brandon McKinney.
    p. cm. -- (Short tales. Norse Myths)
  ISBN 978-1-60270-567-8
  1. Loki (Norse deity)--Juvenile literature. I. McKinney, Brandon, 1970- II. Title.
  BL870.L6W67 2009
  398.209363'01--dc22
                                     2008032539

THE NORSE GODS

ODIN:
The All-Father
of the Gods

FRIGGA:
Queen of
the Gods

BALDUR:
The Best Loved
of the Gods

FORSETI:
God of
Justice

HEIMDALL:
The Guardian
of Asgard

HOD:
God of Winter

THOR:
God of Thunder

TYR:
God of War

HERMOD:
Messenger of
the Gods

FREYR:
God of Weather

LOKI:
The Trickster

FREYA:
Goddess of
Beauty and Love

Mythical Beginnings

Loki goes by many names, including Maker of Lies, Sly God, Shapeshifter, and Trickster.

Loki won many over with his fun-loving ways. At times, he just seemed like a harmless prankster. Often, he used his quick wit to undo the very trouble that he had caused.

As the years went by, Loki's deeds became more serious. He later caused the ruin of Asgard, the land of the gods.

Loki was not a true god. He was a giant.
But unlike most giants, Loki was very handsome.
He was also a gifted speaker.

Loki was married to a fearsome giantess named Angrboda. Together they had three fearsome children.

Their daughter, Hel, became the Goddess of Death.

Loki's two sons were the fiercest creatures ever imagined.

The first was Fenrir, a giant wolf.

The second was Jörmungandr, also known as the Midgard Snake. The Midgard Snake was so large he encircled the earth.

One day, Loki met a traveling god named
Odin. Odin was the greatest of all the gods.

Odin enjoyed Loki's stories very much. The
two made an oath to be brothers.

Loki returned with Odin to Asgard. He lived among the gods as one of them. One day, the gods were discussing a problem.

"The Frost Giants are always trying to enter Asgard," Odin said. "They cause a lot of trouble."

"I know a splendid architect," Loki boasted. "He can build a fortress strong enough to keep the Frost Giants out!"

So, Loki brought them the architect.

"I can build such a fortress," the architect said. "But, my fee will be the sun and the moon."

The gods gasped in shock.

"And the Goddess Freya must become my bride," he added.

"We cannot meet his price," said Baldur.
"But we need the fortress," said Odin.
"Agree to his terms, but tell him he must finish by winter's end or he will receive no payment," Loki said with a grin. "This will be impossible for him!"

The gods were happy to have Loki's wisdom. They did not realize the architect was a Frost Giant. With his giant workhorse, Svadilfare, the architect made quick work of the fortress.

Time quickly passed.

"Winter ends tonight!" Odin exclaimed.

"All that is left is to put a gate on the fortress," Baldur said.

"The architect will easily finish it," Freya said.

"You gave us terrible advice, Loki," Odin said angrily.

"I must not be forced to marry this man," Freya cried.

"We cannot give up the sun and the moon," Thor said.

"You are a fool, Loki!" Baldur yelled.

Loki did not want to be thought of as a fool. He decided to undo his own mischief. He knew the giant needed Svadilfare to finish the gate. So, he came up with a plan.

Loki could change into different things. He made himself into a beautiful mare. Then, he ran across Svadilfare's path.

Svadilfare fell in love with Loki at first sight. He broke free of his harness and chased the mare.

"Come back here!" cried the architect, who ran after the horses.

In the morning, the architect was nowhere to be found. Freya did not have to marry him. The moon and the sun stayed in their places.

The gods finished the fortress on their own. "Your advice was good after all, Loki," said Odin.

"I'm not so sure," said Baldur.

Some time later, Loki saw men attacking Baldur. They used sword and stone against Baldur, but he only laughed.

"Frigga, Queen of the Gods, has protected me from all earthly objects," Baldur said.

Loki learned that Frigga had not protected Baldur from mistletoe.

"Wouldn't you like to join in the fun?" Loki asked one old man. "Use this mistletoe on Baldur. It will merely tickle him."

Everyone watched as the old man tickled Baldur with the mistletoe. They were horrified when Baldur fell dead.

"It was Loki!" the old man cried. "He gave me the mistletoe!"

Loki knew he had gone too far this time. Baldur was everyone's favorite god. Loki ran away, but the other gods soon caught him.

"You must pay for what you've done," Odin said.

The gods chained Loki to a tree. A terrible snake slept in the branches of the tree. Burning venom dripped from the serpent's fangs.

Loki had married a woman in Asgard. His new wife, Sigyn, did what she could to protect Loki. She sat at his side all day long and caught the venom in a cup.

Sometimes Sigyn had to empty the cup. When she left to do this, the horrible venom fell in Loki's eyes. Then, Loki cried out so loudly all of heaven and earth would shake.

One day, Loki escaped. Even though he'd done terrible things, he was angry with the gods. He gathered up his monstrous children, the Frost Giants, and the Fire Giants. They rode toward Asgard.

Loki was no longer interested in pranks. He now meant to destroy all of Asgard.

Heimdall, the Guardian, summoned all the gods into battle. The battle was called Ragnarok. Loki and Heimdall met on the battlefield.

As the flames of Ragnarok died out, a beautiful new world was born. The old gods were gone forever, but the Norse people would always remember Loki. They learned to be watchful of mischief and deceit.